Ready? Set…

go to bed!

Race You to Bed

bob shea

KATHERINE TEGEN BOOKS
An Imprint of HarperCollins Publishers

Up to bed...

down to bed...

All around a goat to bed...

bring a BRING- BRANG- BRUNG to bed!

Grilled cheese to bed!

Angry, angry bees to bed!

But as I say…

as I said…

I'll zip ahead in this race to bed!
'Cause I'm gonna beat you, beat you to bed!

Paddle to bed
with a duck
on my head!

Look! It's Uncle Ted!

Uncle Ted! Uncle Ted!
I'm racing to bed!

Oh no! Over the edge to bed!

Splish to bed... splash to bed!

CAUTION
POISON
IVY

Scratch an itchy rash to bed!

Straight to bed . . .
not late to bed!

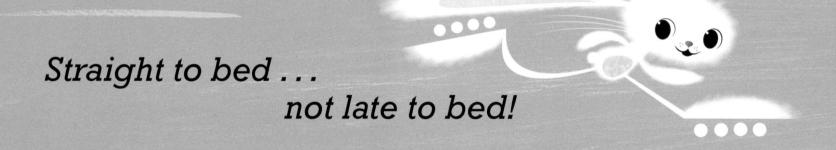

THE AMAZING
HAT
DROP
IT'S NOT A TRICK!

LOOK

WOW

Stop at the drop of a hat to bed!

I'll pick up the pace in this race to bed!

On a car,
on a bus,
on a train
to bed!

Jet to bed to get to bed!
Don't be fooled or misled,
I'm gonna beat you,
beat you to bed!

A snack to bed and a drink to bed,

a bath, a brush, and a book to bed.

Looks like I beat you!

Beat you to bed!

Oh, you're already in bed?
You were way up ahead?

Okay then,
race you to sleep!